Animal Capers

Kerry Argent

Dial Books for Young Readers · New York

Aa

anteater

Bb

bear

Cc

crocodile

Dd

duck

Ee

elephant

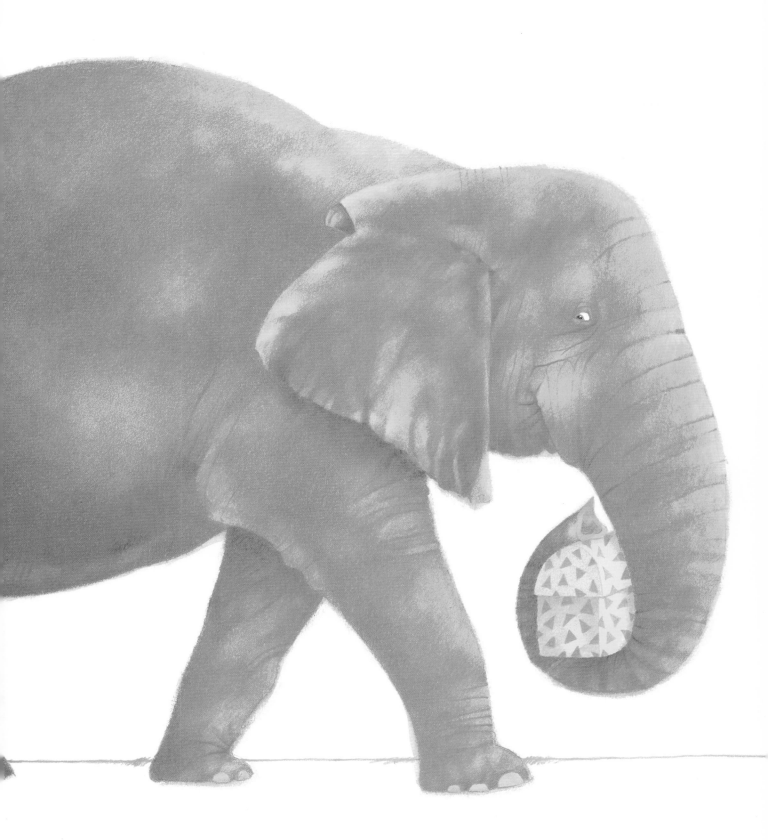

F f

flamingo

G g

gorilla

Hh

hippopotamus

I i

iguana

J j

jaguar

Kk

kookaburra

L l

lion

Mm

monkey

N n

numbat

Oo

otter

P p

peacock

Q q
quail

Rr

rhinoceros

Ss

seal

Tt

tortoise

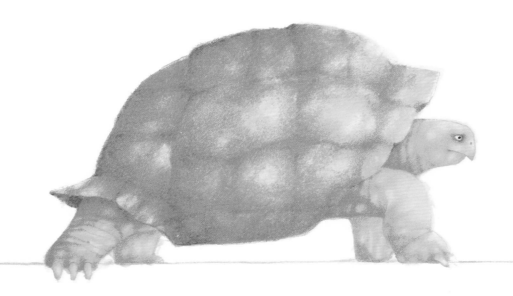

Uu

umbrella bird

V v

vulture

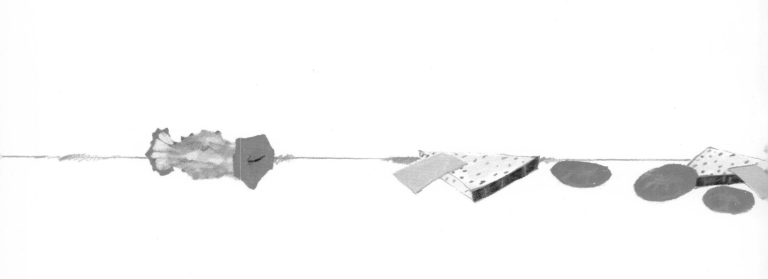

W w

wombat

Xx

x-ray fish

Y y

yak

Zz

zebra

for Rod

First published in the United States 1989
by Dial Books for Young Readers
A Division of Penguin Books USA Inc.
2 Park Avenue
New York, New York 10016

Published simultaneously in Canada by
Fitzhenry & Whiteside Limited, Toronto
Published in Australia by Omnibus Books 1986
in association with Penguin Books Australia Ltd
Illustrations copyright © 1986 by Kerry Argent
All rights reserved
Printed in Hong Kong by
South China Printing Company (1988) Limited
E
2 4 6 8 10 9 7 5 3 1

Library of Congress Cataloging in Publication Data
Argent, Kerry, 1960-
Animal capers / by Kerry Argent.
p. cm.
Summary: Each letter of the alphabet is represented by an animal,
from the anteater and bear to the yak and zebra.
ISBN 0-8037-0718-5.—ISBN 0-8037-0752-5 (lib. bdg.)
1. English language—Alphabet—Juvenile literature.
2. Animals—Juvenile literature. [1. Animals. 2. Alphabet.] I. Title.
PE1155.A74 1990 [E]—dc20 89-33777 CIP AC

The art for this book was created with pastel chalks, ink,
and colored pencils. Each picture was then color-separated
and reproduced in full color.